BLT

Go To The Zoo

Celebrating friendship,
learning, and the magic
of make-believe

The Adventures of BLT - BLT Go To The Zoo
Author: Allison Hoppe
Illustrations: Tabassum Hashmi
Creative Director: David Murack
Interior Layout: Emily Strozinsky
Project Coordinator: Brenda Cortez
Art Coordinator: Jean Sime

ISBN: 979-8-9908071-4-3

Published by Pretty Lake Productions, LLC
Printed in the USA

To my favorite people:

Brooklyn, Lucy, & Theo

● ● ●

My heart and these books are all for you. A huge thank you to
my cousin and creative partner, David Murack. None of this would
be possible without you and I'm forever grateful. And to everyone
who believed in The Adventures of BLT: THANK YOU!

Brooklyn Bacon, Lucy Lettuce, and Theo Tomato are best friends. Every day they go on wonderful adventures together.

Their imaginations run wild, and you
never know what they will come up with next!

• • •

But no matter what, they always have

the best time!

Today was an exciting day:

BLT went to the zoo!

• • •

The zoo was buzzing with excitement.
There were people, fresh popcorn, cotton candy,
and the animals were out and about!

BLT were eager to see all the animals and
learn about their habitats.

"What animal should we
see first?"
asked Theo.

"Let's go see the giraffes!"
said Lucy.

• • •

Along the way they stopped
to get some popcorn.

They arrived to see a baby giraffe and her mom.

The baby stuck her snout through the cage, grabbed some of Lucy's popcorn and ate it!

"She must be hungry for a snack!"
laughed Lucy.

"I wonder what other kinds of food giraffes like?"

"We like leaves up in the trees, twigs, grass, fruits, and roots. I'm not supposed to eat popcorn, but it sure is tasty!" said the baby giraffe.

"How much do you usually eat?"
asked Lucy.

"Up to 75 pounds a day!"
she exclaimed.

"That would be a lot of popcorn!"
laughed Lucy. "Thanks for teaching us, next time I'll sneak you in an apple!"

● ● ●

"I'd like that!" she replied.

BLT headed towards the monkeys next.

• • •

"Monkeys are my favorite animal.
I love how they swing and climb
from tree to tree."

Theo said.

MONKEYS

"Wow! They look like they are flying!"
shouted Lucy.

"They move so fast,"
said Brooklyn.

"Would you like to hold one?" asked the zookeeper.

"Yes please!"

Theo said with excitement.

"His name is Rizzo," she said.

Rizzo climbed around on Theo's shoulders and started picking through his hair, tickling his head.

• • •

Theo started laughing and asked what Rizzo was doing.

"I'm grooming you!"

said Rizzo.

"Monkeys and other primates groom each other to form bonds. It's a sign that we like you. You don't have that much hair to groom!"

"This feels so good I could fall asleep," sighed Theo.

Rizzo whispered, "It's meant to be relaxing!"

• • •

"Come back anytime for a head scratch!"

smiled Rizzo.

"Thank you, I sure will,"

replied Theo.

"I'd really like to see the penguins,"
said Brooklyn.

• • •

BLT walked on over to the exhibit. When they got there, they saw a group of penguins playing.

PENGUINS

"They are so cute!
Look at their white bellies,"
shouted Theo.

"I like how they teeter-tot
when they walk,"
said Lucy.

"I wonder how cold the
water is?"
asked Brooklyn.

As they were observing the penguins,
one climbed to the top of a rock and slid down
on his belly, diving into the water.

Water splashed everywhere!

"Now I know how cold the water is.
It's really, really cold!"
shivered Brooklyn.

"I don't think I'd like being a penguin."

"I splashed you pretty good,"
said the penguin.

"Lots of us live in Antarctica. We can swim in water as cold as 28 degrees Fahrenheit."

"That is so cold," said Brooklyn. "How do you do it?"

"Our body temperature is between 100-102 degrees, and our feathers add an extra layer that keeps us warm," explained the penguin.

• • •

"Wow! Thanks for teaching us about penguins,"
said Brooklyn.

"No problem, stay warm!"
replied the penguin.

"Can you believe giraffes can eat 75 pounds a day!"

asked Lucy.

"Or that monkeys clean each other!"

said Theo.

"And that penguins swim in ice cold water!"

exclaimed Brooklyn.

"We have a lot more
to learn next time,"

said Lucy.

They put their hands together and chanted...

• • •

BLT! BLT! BLT!

Find BLT & Friends

The adventure continues! Help to find BLT and their friends that are lost in the jungle, out in the savanna, and in Antarctica!

about the author

Allison Hoppe is the author of *The Adventures of BLT*.
Her work is inspired by her nieces and nephew, Brooklyn, Lucy,
& Theo. When Allison is not writing, she is going on adventures
with the real BLT, traveling, learning, and ever-evolving.